THOMAS THE TANK ENGINE & FRIENDS ANNUAL

Based on The Railway Series by The Rev. W. Awdry

Written by Christopher Awdry
Text © William Heinemann Limited 1988

End paper illustration by Owain Bell
© William Heinemann Limited 1986

Other full colour illustrations by David Palmer
© William Heinemann Limited 1988

Line illustrations by Sheila Bedwell
© William Heinemann Limited 1987

Photographic stills by David Mitton and Terry Permane
from the TV series
"Thomas The Tank Engine and Friends"
© Britt Allcroft (Thomas) Limited 1984, 1986

Published by

GRANDREAMS LIMITED
Jadwin House, 205/211 Kentish Town Road,
London NW5 2JU.

Printed in Spain.

ISBN 0 86227 635 7

CONTENTS

Hello!

"…well, I don't think it's right, Ben."

"There's not much you can do about it, Bill."

"No, but it's the principle of it. I don't…oh, er…hello. Sorry, didn't realise you'd come in. Mr. Awdry said you would, but that's what I'm on about. We've been blacklettered…"

"Blackmailed, Bill."

"That's what I said."

"No you didn't, you said…"

"Oh never mind, stop arguing in front of all these people. Now, where was I? Ah, yes, we've been blackmailed because that Mr. Awdry told us that if we would introduce this Annual for Thomas,

he would write a story about us in it."

"Who, Thomas? I didn't know he could write."

"Not Thomas, silly, Mr. Awdry."

"But Mr. Awdry has written a story about us, Bill."

"Yes, but we don't come into it much."

"What more do you want? Anyway, if you keep on the right side of him he might do a whole book about us."

"I never thought of that. Do you think he would?"

"He certainly won't if you keep moaning about him."

"No. But there's another thing. He

6

said he'd tell the readers about our friends the twin engines in Cornwall, but he hasn't. Do you think we ought to instead?"

"That's true — good idea, Bill. Judy and Alfred they're called. I wonder if Alfred is working yet?"

"I expect so, Ben. The people at the Bodmin & Wenford Railway will be looking after him properly, I'm sure, and if you readers want to see him, you can find him at a place called Bodmin."

"And Judy is at a museum near St. Austell. It's a fascinating place Mr. Awdry says, where you can climb a hill and watch china clay actually being washed out of the ground, and…"

"Er…Ben?"

"Yes, Bill?"

"Why don't you stop chattering and let everyone get on with reading the Annual?"

"Chattering? Me?"

"Uh-huh. There are lots of new stories about Thomas and his friends…"

"…and us — don't forget us. And colouring and puzzles and a game."

"That's right. Turn the page and enjoy it — we're sure you will."

TRAPPED BY TREES

The wind moaned through the smoke-vents in the roof of the big engine shed at Tidmouth. Now and then the moan became a whistle during the stronger gusts. The engines listened anxiously.

"I hope it doesn't blow the signals down, like it did that time when we all had to be flag-signalled through Knapford," said Henry nervously.

James, who had learned a lesson that day, agreed.

But the wind had not lessened by the morning.

"Ouch!" exclaimed Henry as he came out of the Shed. "I don't like this."

"Pooh!" scoffed Gordon. "Not scared of a bit of wind are you? Whatever would happen to my Express if I let a little bit of wind bother me?"

"Well, you just be careful," retorted Henry. "I expect the bell on the viaduct is ringing like mad today."

The Fat Controller had had an instrument fitted to the viaduct. Driven by the wind, this rang a warning bell in the nearest station to each end when the wind was too strong for trains to cross safely.

"Pooh!" said Gordon again. "I've no time to worry about that."

His outward journey went well in spite of the wind, but it was stronger by the time he set out for home, and he began to regret his boastful words. But at the station before the viaduct the signals were clear.

"That's all right, Gordon," said his driver. "Away we go, but I think we'll cross as fast as we can, just in case."

Gordon was still anxious, but then he remembered his passengers and what he had said to the others that morning.

"I daren't stop now," he thought. "They'll laugh at me."

When they reached the viaduct

Gordon was glad they were going fast — the wind funnelling up the valley hit them like a sledgehammer.

"Ooof!" spluttered Gordon. It felt as if the whole viaduct was rocking, not just him and his train. "Hurry, hurry, hurry!" he panted bravely, and heaved a great sigh of relief when he reached the other side safely.

The Hill, where he had stuck many

years before, was sheltered from the wind, but when they reached Edward's station they came to a signal at danger.

"There's a tree down across your track," the stationmaster explained, "but the other line is clear, so if you push your train back to the crossover we can get you past 'wrong line'."

"Bother!" said Gordon. "We shall be late now."

"Can't be helped," said his driver, and he put his hand on Gordon's reverser. As he did so there was an extra fierce gust of wind. A tree at the end of the platform, just clear of the last coach, creaked, groaned and fell with a sickening crash, right across the points Gordon wanted to use. Gordon was moving only slowly, so he had no difficulty in stopping.

"That's torn it," said the fireman. "We're trapped. Don't worry, Gordon. Nobody's going anywhere for a bit."

The stationmaster ran to the telephone and Gordon and his passengers waited. They didn't have very long to wait, really, but to Gordon it seemed like ages before he heard a cheerful whistle from the station yard.

"Hullo, Gordon," called Trevor. "Trapped by trees, are you? Never mind — we'll soon have you out. What a bit of luck I was sawing logs when the stationmaster telephoned, so I had steam up and all my gear ready."

Trevor was as good as his word. While he was working, Henry came by and saw Gordon's predicament. He didn't say anything — he just smiled to himself.

Gordon was soon free. He thanked Trevor for rescuing him, and backed his coaches carefully over the cleared points. With a cheerful "toot, toot" Trevor chuffered off to deal with the second tree.

It was very late when Gordon reached the Big Station, but the passengers understood, and didn't complain. As he went back to the Shed for a rest the wind suddenly died away to a whisper.

"Wind!" muttered Gordon crossly. "Bah!"

A picture to colour.

15

James

JAMES (Number 5) is the only red engine on the Fat Controller's Railway — red with gold stripes — which has sometimes made him think he is more important than the others. He has the same number of wheels as Edward, but they are arranged differently — two small wheels in front, and six big wheels, though they are not as big as Henry's or Gordon's. He is a 'mixed-traffic' engine, which means he should be able to pull trucks just as easily as coaches. But James has had trouble with trucks. He is sometimes rude to them, and the trucks don't like it and try to catch him out.

Find The Engines

Illustrated on the opposite page are 10 characters associated with The Railway Series. If you put their names in the correct order in the grid provided, the names of 2 more engines will be found in the heavier ruled boxes. Answers on pages 60-61.

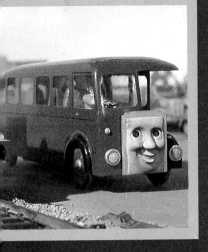

Find The Engines

Thomas's driver held a newspaper in his hand.

"There's a stray dog chasing sheep in the valley," he remarked. "Let's hope it's caught before any harm is done."

The fireman agreed, but Thomas wasn't worried.

"Dogs don't bother me," he thought. "I'd just blow steam at him, like Toby did with that bull. That would soon show him what's what."

The signal arm dropped, and Thomas set off happily with Annie and Clarabel. Beyond the tunnel the valley became wider. Bertie came towards them along the nearby road, and Thomas whistled cheerfully. Bertie tooted in return, and his driver waved to them from his window.

A little way along the line Thomas heard a dog barking — it seemed to come from ahead. He took no notice at first, until suddenly, a short distance in front, the hedge beside the line seemed to bulge towards them. A sheep appeared, struggling, another jumped over it and ran onto the track, and all at once a small flock seemed to overflow across the line. A black and white dog followed, barking furiously.

"Whoa, Thomas," called his driver, but Thomas didn't need telling. With a grinding of brakes he came to a standstill as quickly as he could. Several passengers looked out of the carriage windows to see what was happening.

The dog stopped barking. Thomas found that he didn't need to blow steam at him. As soon as the dog saw Thomas, it turned and ran quickly through the gap in the hedge and across the field.

But the poor sheep, thoroughly confused and frightened, didn't know what to do. Some ran along the line, some stood quivering with fright, while others, braver than the rest, just went a little way off and began to eat the grass

OUT! SHEEP

on the cutting.

"I know whose sheep these are," said the fireman. "He lives just over there — I'll nip across and get help."

He was soon back with a shepherd and two sheepdogs. In next to no time they had rounded up the sheep and guided them back through the gap in the hedge into their field.

Meanwhile, the Guard had been making sure nothing ran into the train. He came back just as Thomas's driver and fireman were climbing back into their cab, and the last sheep was disappearing through the hedge.

"Right, Thomas," said his driver. "Away we go."

But Thomas couldn't move.

"My wheels won't turn," he complained.

"Something's wrong with the brakes," said the fireman.

"Bother!" said the Guard when they told him. "Now I shall have to go all the way back to the signalbox again to tell them we can't move yet after all. Can you fix it, or do you want me to ask for a fitter?"

"We'll try," said the fireman, and while the Guard trudged back along the line once more, he and the driver got down and set to work.

Thomas waited thoughtfully for a while, but soon became impatient. He seemed to have been waiting for ages, though it was really only about ten minutes.

"Are we ever going to start?" he thought crossly.

Suddenly he heard a shout from his driver.

"Got it," he called, and went to work with a spanner. "A brake-pipe had worked loose when we stopped suddenly," he explained as he climbed back into the cab. "We'll be all right now."

There was a hiss, and Thomas felt the brakes come off.

"Right," said the driver, opening the regulator to let steam into Thomas's cylinders. "Away we go."

"Get a move on, get a move on," puffed Thomas impatiently.

"Wait-a-min-ute, wait-a-min-ute," wailed Clarabel, but Thomas was in a hurry and took no notice. He had lost enough time already, and wanted to make up some of it.

The next station was by the river. While the passengers got in, Thomas's driver told the Stationmaster what had happened.

"Come along," Thomas hissed impatiently.

"We can't, Thomas," said the driver.

"We haven't had the 'all clear' from the Guard yet..." He suddenly stopped and clapped his hand to his forehead.

"Crumbs!" he exclaimed. "We must have left him behind."

They had, and of course they had to wait for him to catch up. He was very cross and very tired when he did.

"I'm sorry, Mr. Guard," said Thomas. "Clarabel did tell me to wait, but I wanted to make up lost time. And now I've lost even more," he finished sadly.

"Never mind, Thomas," said the Guard. "It was that wretched dog's fault really. The signalman told me that the farmer had caught him, so we'll have no more trouble. Let's move off quickly and hope we don't meet sheep anywhere else."

There are 5 differences between these two pictures. Can you spot them? Answers on pages 60-61.

EDWARD is engine number 2, and has his number painted on his tender. Like Thomas he is blue with red stripes, but he has more wheels than Thomas — four small ones in front, and four bigger ones behind, which drive him along. He also has his own branch line, running to the port where Bill and Ben work. Perhaps his proudest moment was when he helped to rescue James from running away. He had a sort of race with Bertie too, but he didn't know that Bertie was trying to catch up with him. And do you remember who came to the rescue when Gordon got stuck on the hill . . ?

Edward

A picture to colour.

GORDON is very big and very proud. At first he was the only engine strong enough to pull the Express, and he knew it. Now he knows better, but it doesn't stop him boasting now and then. He is blue with red stripes, and carries the number 4 on his tender. He has more wheels than any of the others — more, even, than Henry, because he has an extra pair of small wheels behind his six big ones. Gordon doesn't like goods trains, and once got so cross when he was asked to pull one that he ran off a turntable into a ditch. Can you remember who pulled him out?

Gordon

POST EARLY FOR CHRISTMAS

Christmas was coming. All the letters, cards and parcels posted in Ffarquhar were carried along Thomas's branch line to the sorting office in Tidmouth. The trains became heavier and heavier.

One day, about a week before Christmas, the people at the Post Office in Ffarquhar asked for a special train that evening. The Stationmaster agreed and arranged for Percy to take it.

That was during the morning. About lunchtime the sky clouded over, thick and heavy from the east. It began to snow, not hard at first, but by teatime it had turned into a blizzard.

Percy shivered.

"Just my luck to have to go out again," he grumbled. "I'd much rather be in my nice warm shed."

"Wouldn't we all," agreed his driver and fireman, "but orders are orders. You wouldn't want children missing their presents on Christmas Day just because you'd rather be in a shed, would you?"

They fixed the snowplough to Percy's front bufferbeam. When all the mail, in sacks, and packed in big metal trolleys, had been loaded onto the train, Percy set off.

Rather to his surprise the snow wasn't too bad. The tunnel was usually the worst place in snow, but they reached it without trouble. Percy whistled cheerfully as they passed Mrs Kyndley's cottage, but nobody waved in reply. Crimson curtains were sensibly drawn against the weather, and a warm glow of light shone through them onto the snow outside.

"We'll be all right now," said the fireman, as they came safely out into the valley. But he was wrong.

They passed the station by the river all right, but they found in the open land lower down the valley that the snow had drifted more deeply. Conditions became steadily worse. Before they reached the station by the airfield they realised that they could go no further. By now the snow was level with Percy's buffers, and a sharp wind was blowing snow off the sides of the cutting to pile up around him.

"Quick," urged Percy's driver. "Back to the last station or we shall be stranded!"

But it was too late. Already the snow was so thick around Percy's wheels that they just spun helplessly and didn't move him an inch.

"Go back to the station and tell them what has happened," the driver told the fireman. "Thank goodness there aren't any passengers to worry about."

"No," grumbled the fireman. "Only me. You didn't say I'd need snowshoes, did you." He told the guard where he was going, and a little while later the guard came to Percy's cab to be near the fire. He rubbed his hands together happily.

"Make the most of it," remarked the driver with a grin. "We can only keep it going as long as the coal and water lasts."

When the fireman reached the station the staff there wasted no time in sending for help. But the weather was worse on the coast, and even Donald and Douglas couldn't force their way through. They thought of sending to Ffarquhar for Thomas, but then realised that by the time he could reach them the snow would probably be thick enough to strand him too.

They held a conference in the Stationmaster's office.

"It's the mail that is the biggest worry," said the Stationmaster. "We can't just leave it stuck in the snow."

32

"Don't they keep part of the airfield clear at all times?" suggested Percy's fireman. "Harold the Helicopter's here, he could take the mail for us."

"They'd never let him take off in this blizzard," objected the Stationmaster.

They took hot drinks and food down to Percy's driver and guard, and, in several journeys, brought the sacks of mail up to the station. Early next morning the skies had cleared enough for Harold to be allowed to take off. He took as many sacks as he could, and kept coming back for more until the mail was cleared.

It was afternoon before Thomas and Toby reached them from Ffarquhar, and they pulled Percy and his train back to safety.

"Thank you for rescuing me," said Percy. "Now I know what you felt like Thomas. Remember that year when you went to collect the Christmas tree for the Fat Controller and you became stranded in the snow blizzard and you had to be rescued? It was all right until my fire went out, but I don't want to do it again. Next year, posting early for Christmas can start as soon as it likes!"

Word Search

Hidden in the grid below are the 30 words
shown at the bottom of the page. How many
can you find? Answers on pages 60-61.

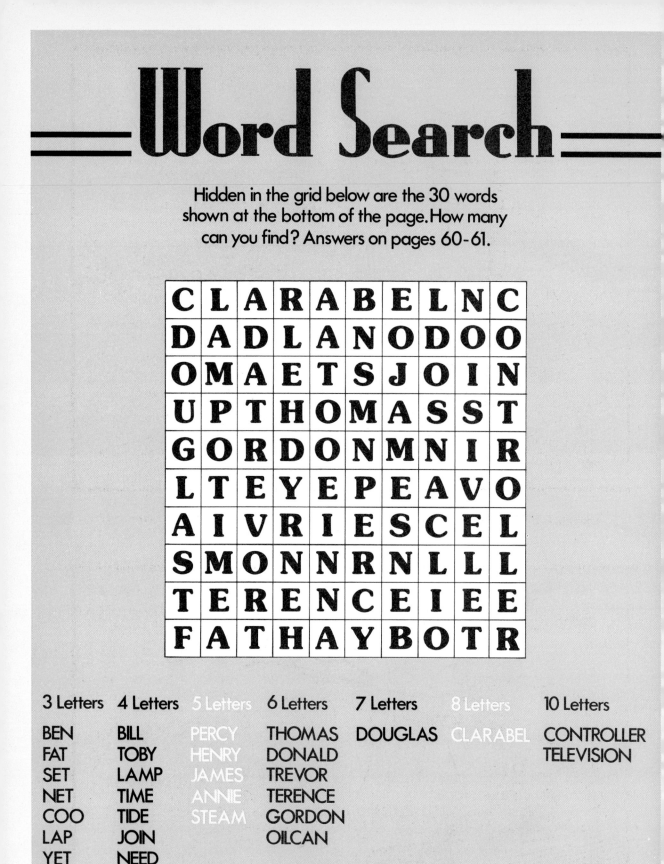

```
C L A R A B E L N C
D A D L A N O D O O
O M A E T S J O I N
U P T H O M A S S T
G O R D O N M N I R
L T E Y E P E A V O
A I V R I E S C E L
S M O N N R N L L L
T E R E N C E I E E
F A T H A Y B O T R
```

3 Letters	4 Letters	5 Letters	6 Letters	7 Letters	8 Letters	10 Letters
BEN	BILL	PERCY	THOMAS	DOUGLAS	CLARABEL	CONTROLLER
FAT	TOBY	HENRY	DONALD			TELEVISION
SET	LAMP	JAMES	TREVOR			
NET	TIME	ANNIE	TERENCE			
COO	TIDE	STEAM	GORDON			
LAP	JOIN		OILCAN			
YET	NEED					
HAY						

There are 5 differences between these two pictures. Can you spot them? Answers on pages 60-61.

BERTIE has been on the Island of Sodor for many years. Thomas was stuck in the snow when Bertie first met him — he took Thomas's passengers while Terence pulled him free. After their race Thomas and Bertie became good friends, and now each brings passengers for the other. Bertie was able to help in a rather different way once. He had taken a party of Sunday School children to the seaside, when one of the teachers was taken ill. In much less time than it would have taken an ambulance, Bertie took her straight to the hospital, where she soon got well again.

Bertie

A picture to colour.

39

HAROLD AND THE LANDSLIDE

When it rained the other engines sometimes teased Duck.

"This sort of weather ought to suit you," they said, and Duck would laugh with them.

But he didn't really like rain any more than they did, and now and then he was tempted to hide in the tunnel on his branch line, and wait until the rain had stopped. Then he remembered what had happened to Henry many years before, and knew that it would be silly. Besides,

he always had passengers who wanted to reach their destinations and would be cross if they didn't. Not to mention the Fat Controller.

One autumn the rain seemed to go on for ever. Day after day it poured; great pools of water spread over the fields, and all the rivers and streams were full to overflowing. Few passengers ventured out unless they had to, so Duck was surprised one morning when a party of young men, carrying packs on their backs,

40

travelled from Tidmouth to Arlesburgh.

"Hikers," explained Duck's driver. "Probably on holiday, so they don't want to waste their time, even if it is raining."

By the time Duck set out for Tidmouth again it seemed to be raining harder than ever. They had not gone far when Duck noticed that the rails didn't seem to be there any more! His driver noticed too — luckily, because the rain made it difficult to see properly, they were not going fast and could stop easily. As they watched, part of the embankment slithered sideways and more rails disappeared.

"Back, Duck, back!" urged his driver. Duck didn't need telling twice.

When they were once more on solid ground they stopped again, and the Guard ran to the nearest signal-box to explain what had happened. Then they got permission to return to the station.

A little later the Stationmaster came running on to the platform.

"Emergency!" he told them. "One of those hikers has been caught in a landslide on the cliffs and needs the hospital. But the road is out as well as the railway, and it will take ages for an ambulance to come the long way round.

"Sounds like a job for Harold," remarked Duck.

The Stationmaster stared.

"Of course," he said. "Well done, Duck — it's a good job you haven't let the rain send *your* brain rusty."

He ran at once to telephone the airfield.

"Ugh!" said Harold when he heard the news. "But we can't leave the poor chap there for even more landslides to fall on him, can we."

Quickly he was into the air and away, and though the wind was against him, it wasn't long before they reached the place.

The hikers had been walking along a cliff path. Part of it had collapsed and slipped down the cliffside, taking one of the hikers with it. Luckily a ledge lower down had prevented him from going too far, but the fall had broken one of his arms, and in any case the cliff was too steep for him to have climbed back up.

Harold hovered anxiously a few feet above the injured man, and as close to the cliff as he dared. He was very careful, because near cliffs there can be sudden winds which might blow an unwary helicopter into trouble. Harold could feel that the gusts were becoming stronger.

Very cautiously, a rescue officer was winched down on a strong cable. The injured hiker was helped on to a special stretcher, and when he had been securely strapped to it, he was pulled up into Harold.

Then the cable was let down again, so that the rescue officer could be pulled up too. When he was safely inside, Harold breathed a sigh of relief.

"Phew!" he said. "Thank goodness that's done. Quick, let's get away from these cliffs before the wind blows any harder."

But once above the cliff the wind helped, and before long they were hovering above the hospital at Wellsworth. They landed gently on a lawn near the car-park, and the hiker was taken into safe hands, to have his arm put into plaster.

"Well done Harold," said the Doctor. "Our young friend's accident has spoilt his holiday, but thanks to you he'll soon be . . . " — he broke off and glanced up at the sky — " . . . as right as rain, I suppose."

As for Duck, he had a holiday too; he was stuck at Arlesdale for a week while the line was repaired. The passengers had a long journey by bus, but poor Duck couldn't go anywhere. He says he doesn't want another holiday — they're too boring.

Word Place

Place the words listed below in the grid shown.
Answers on pages 60-61.

2 Letters	3 Letters		4 Letters	5 Letters	6 Letters	7 Letters	8 Letters
ME	OUT	GAS	TOBY	RAILS	DONALD	POSTMAN	ODDITIES
	TOO	NIP	LAMB	NIGHT	TREVOR		
	ALL	EBB	BOCO	CAMEO			
	MOP	BAR		YACHT			
	RAN	RAT					
	PAT						

Henry

HENRY is green, with red stripes. It was because he didn't want to get his paint wet that he once went into a tunnel and stayed there. Henry's number is 3, and he has ten wheels — four small ones in front and six driving wheels, like Thomas. He hasn't always been the same shape though — once he had an accident while pulling a fish train, and the Fat Controller sent him away to be rebuilt. They gave him a bigger firebox at the same time, and now he can pull the Express easily: Gordon is sometimes jealous that he does it so well. Here is Henry before his accident.

47

1. What colour is Henry?

Railway Quiz

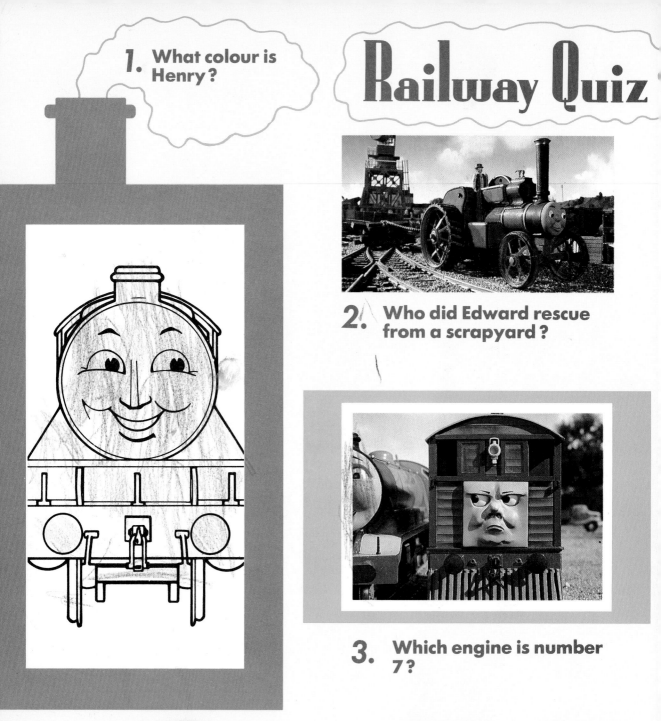

2. Who did Edward rescue from a scrapyard?

3. Which engine is number 7?

4. Who ran off a turntable into a ditch because he didn't want to pull a special train?

5. And who pulled him out of it?

Railway Quiz Railway Quiz

6. Where did Henry (above) go to be mended after his accident?

7. Who gave Thomas a branch line as a reward for becoming a Really Useful Engine?

8. How many wheels have Donald and Douglas got each?

9. Which engine was once frightened by a bull?

10. What number is Gordon?

ANSWERS ON PAGES 60/61

QUICK THINKING

Bill and Ben were feeling rushed off their wheels. The china clay pits where they worked became busier and busier as more people asked for it.

"All this fuss about a bit of earth," grumbled Bill as he and Ben rolled wearily into their shed one night. "Don't know what they see in it. What on earth do they want it for, I'd like to know."

His driver laughed.

"China clay is special," he said. "People are finding they can use it in all sorts of things."

"What sorts of things?" demanded Ben.

"Well, pottery, of course," said Bill's driver. "And paper, paints, rubber, plastics, medicines, fertilisers..." He paused.

"Is that all?" asked Bill.

"Good gracious, no," said his driver in surprise. "I still haven't mentioned..."

"Stop," pleaded Ben, "you're making my head spin."

The drivers laughed again, and went home to tea.

Every day Donald, Douglas or BoCo came to the station at the end of Edward's branch line to collect a trainload of clay trucks, or 'hoods' as the men called them. The first time he came BoCo had wanted to know why.

"They're full of dried clay," Bill and Ben had explained importantly. "The hoods are those pointed covers that keep it dry if it rains. Wet clay is much heavier and has to go in special tank wagons."

One day when Donald arrived there were more trucks than he could take in one journey.

"BoCo is following with some more empties," he explained to Bill and Ben.

"He'll take the rest away for you, and I'm to wait at Edward's station to help him up Gordon's Hill when he pulls them all to the Mainland."

Donald took as many as he thought he could manage. It might have been better if he had been more cautious.

About halfway along the branch line is a passing loop, at the bottom of a short but quite steep hill. At the top of the hill

Donald tried to put on his brakes, but the trucks surged against him. They took him by surprise and gave him a fearful bump. He tried to stop, but as more trucks ran on to the slope of the hill they pushed harder and harder, so that Donald began to gather speed.

"Help, help!" he whistled. "Stupid things — stop pushing."

The trucks took no notice.

"On, on, on," they laughed, and pushed harder still.

Poor Donald was desperate. Sparks flew from his brake blocks, but he couldn't stop the trucks. Then he whistled again in alarm, for beyond the loop, coming towards him, he saw BoCo with his empty trucks.

"Horrors!" he whistled. "How am I going to stop to let him past?"

The two engines reached the loop at the same time, but by now BoCo, with the shorter train, was going faster. He hoped so anyway. Whistling desperately Donald shot past, his driver still fighting to bring the trucks under control.

BoCo heard Donald's whistle and gave an answering toot on his horn. Then he noticed the sparks coming from Donald's brakes.

"Donald's in trouble!" he gasped. "If he's running away, he'll never be able to stop in the loop and he'll hit us head-on for sure."

BoCo's driver pushed the throttle wide open.

"Quick," he said. "Our train is short enough for the loop — we don't know about Donald's. We might just make it into our side so that he can have a clear run through."

Leaving it as late as he dared, BoCo's driver brought him safely to a halt, just as Donald crossed the points at the other end, missing BoCo's Guard's van by inches.

"Phew!" remarked BoCo when he had recovered his breath. "That was close."

When BoCo eventually reached Edward's station with the rest of the clay 'hoods', Donald was waiting.

"Thank you for thinking so quickly," he said. "You saved a nasty accident."

BoCo smiled.

"You had me worried for a bit," he said. "Lucky my train was a short one, or I don't know what might have happened."

"I do," said Donald, "but I'd rather not think about it."

Draw the picture of James in the space below, using the squares as a guide. Then colour in both pictures.

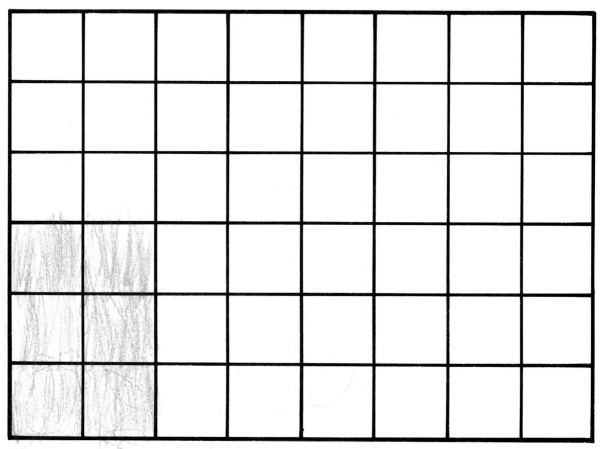

Draw the picture of Percy and Harold in the space below, using the squares as a guide. Then colour in both pictures.

Thomas

THOMAS is a small engine with six wheels. He is blue, with red stripes, and has his number, 1, on his water-tank each side. He is a tank engine, which means he can carry coal and water with him instead of needing a tender like the bigger engines. As a reward for proving himself a Really Useful Engine the Fat Controller gave him a branch line all to himself. He has had many adventures — a race with Bertie the bus, he got himself stuck in the snow and had to be pulled out, he got fish in his water-tank, and he fell down a mine. Can you think of any others?

Answers

Word Place

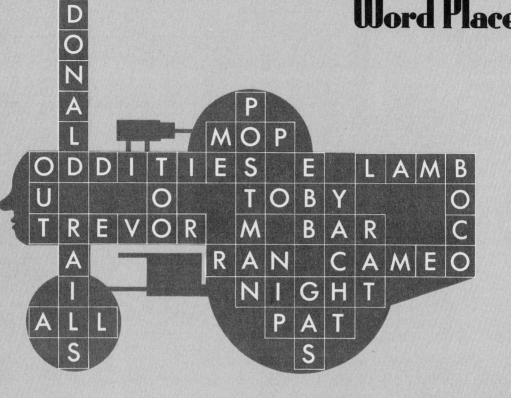

Word Search

Let as

Railway Quiz

1. Green
2. Trevor
3. Toby
4. Gordon
5. James and Henry
6. Crewe
7. The Fat Controller
8. 6
9. Daisy
10. 4

Find The Engines

Spot The Difference